SECRET AGENT MOLE

To Graeme, Simon and Poppy -JF

Published in the UK by Scholastic, 2024
1 London Bridge, London, SE1 9BG
Scholastic Ireland, 89E Lagan Road, Dublin Industrial Estate,
Glasnevin, Dublin, D11 HP5F

First published in Australia by Scholastic Australia, 2023

Book design by Hannah Janzen

ISBN 978 0702 33131 2

A CIP catalogue record for this book is available from the British Library.

Printed and bound in Great Britain by Clays Ltd, Elcograf S.p.A
Paper made from wood grown in sustainable forests and other controlled sources.

1 3 5 7 9 10 8 6 4 2

www.scholastic.co.uk

JAMES FOLEY

SECRET AGENT MOLE

GOLDFISH-FINGER

CHAPTER ONE:
MOLE ON A MISSION

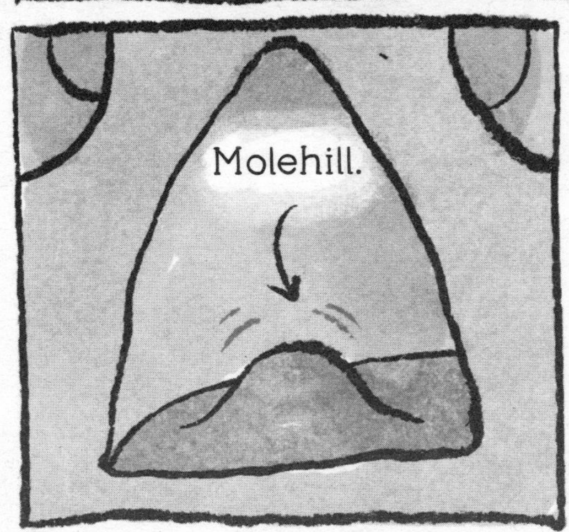

FLIP!

All clear.

HNGNN!

Hippo.
Helena Hippo.

You could've dug the tunnel a bit wider, Max. I'm a little larger than you.
Sorry, Helena, I didn't think. I'm too excited. It's our very first mission!

I've dreamed of this since I was a baby mole.

SLURP

You've got to think ahead, Max.
You can't go running headfirst into danger without a plan.
But I *have* a plan.

Step 1: Tunnel into the bad guy's secret lair.
Tick!

Step 2:
Find the bad guy.

Step 3:
Introduce him to Mr Boom-Boom here.
Mission complete!

That's not a very detailed plan.
Well, *I'm* the team leader and I say the plan will work . . .

... and if it doesn't, that's why *you're* here. You're the muscle.
One look at you and the bad guy will give up.

True. I am formidable.
And if *you* can't defeat him ...
BZZZZZZZ

BZZZZZZZzz
BZZZZZZzz
… then that's why *Bug* is here. She's the brains.
Bug. June Bug.
What do you mean, 'you can smell earthworms on my breath?'

Come on, Max, you know how important this mission is.
We need to get this right . . .
We'll be fine. Now, let's find our bad guy. He's not gonna know what hit him . . .

BOOM

DR NUDE!

In the flesh.
And *you* are?

A high-tech cockroach? Disgusting.
Luckily, I always keep bug spray handy.
COUGH! COUGH!
A muscly hippo?
You're no match for my mecha-suit.
BOOT
OOF!

And—haha—
a *mole*?
Takes
one to know
one.

I'm a
naked mole *rat*,
not a *mole*.
There's a
difference.

Clearly
the difference
is *pants*.

GRR!
BOOM!
FLOOP!

PLOP!
Temper, temper,
Rudie Nudie.
Quiet,
rodent!
THWACK
OOF!

What is that beetle babbling about?

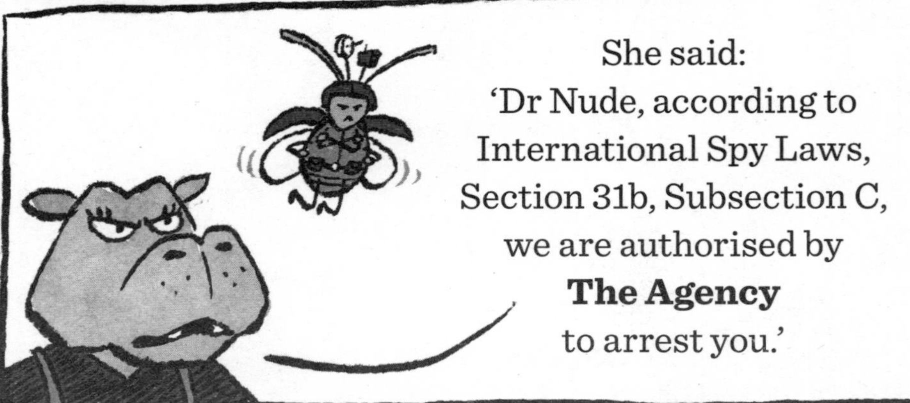
She said:
'Dr Nude, according to International Spy Laws, Section 31b, Subsection C, we are authorised by **The Agency** to arrest you.'

And how will you stop me, Hippo? With your muscles?
If I have to.
Well, before you do . . .
BEEP
. . . say hello to my guests.
CRACK

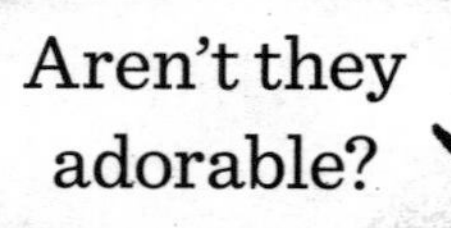
Aren't they adorable?
I kitten-napped them from the orphanage this morning.
The only thing stopping them from falling into the pit of spikes . . .
. . . is the claw holding on to that cable.

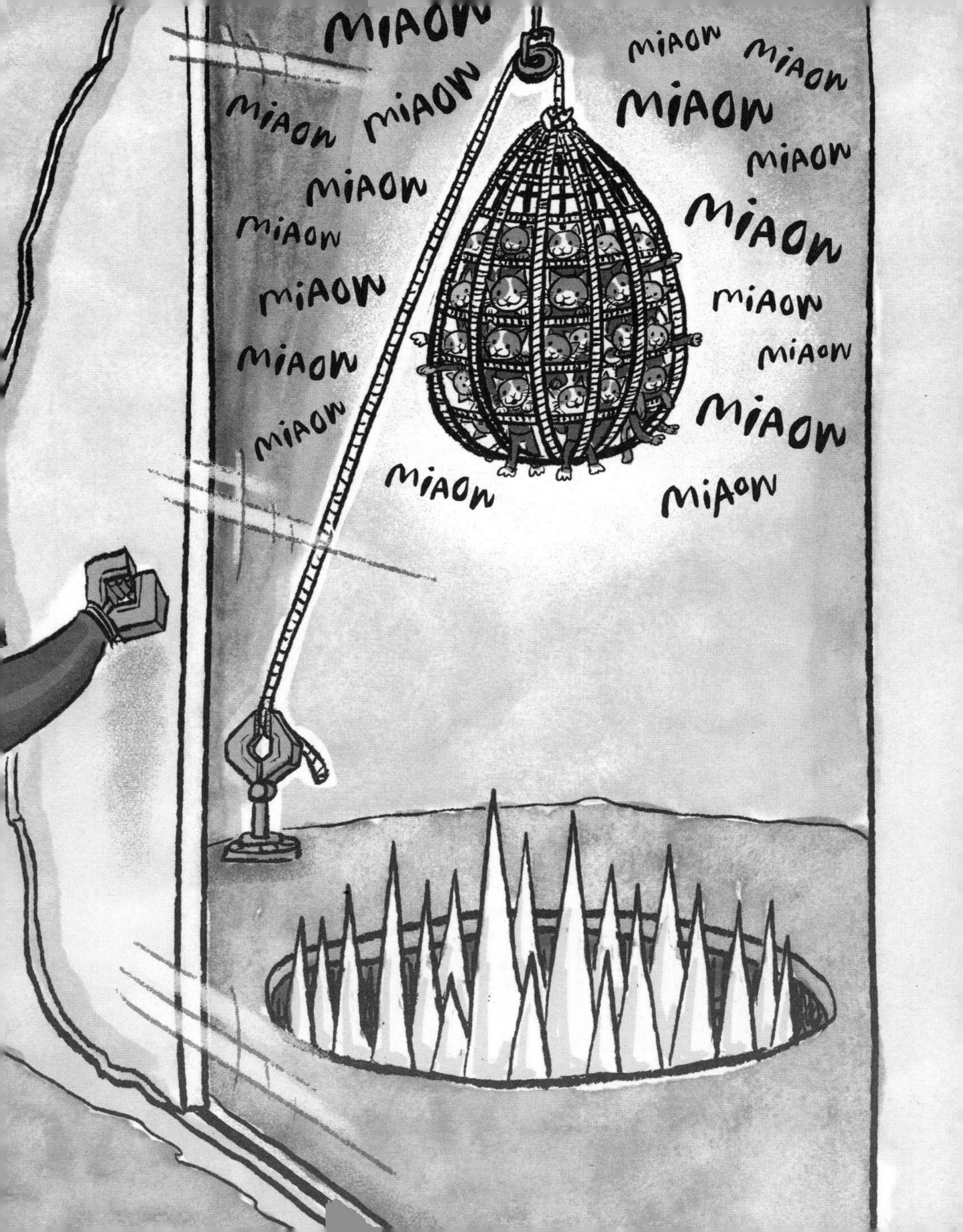
MIAOW
MIAOW
MIAOW
MIAOW
MIAOW
MIAOW
MIAOW
MIAOW
MIAOW
MIAOW
MIAOW
MIAOW
MIAOW
MIAOW
MIAOW
MIAOW
MIAOW
MIAOW

Better
hurry, Hippo—
those kittens won't
save themselves.

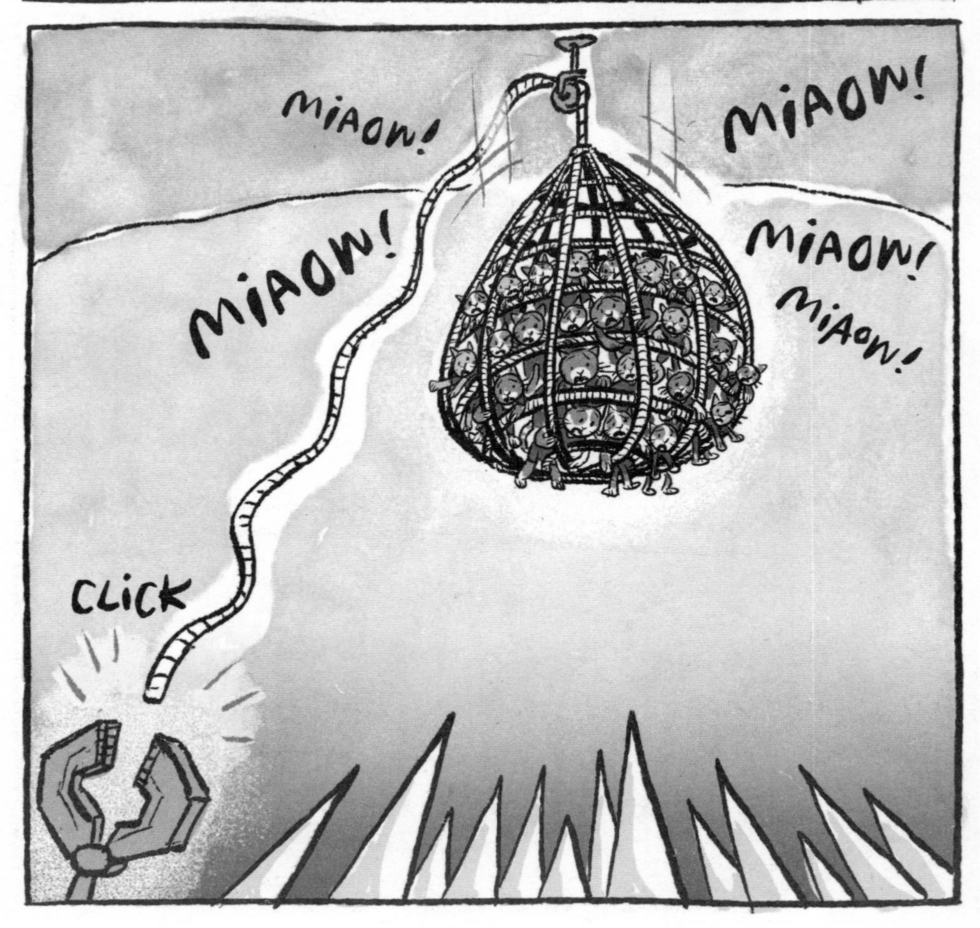

No!
LEAP!

Gotcha!

Oh no.
I just remembered.
I'm allergic to cats.
SPROING!!
YAY!

You won't get away with this, Nudie!
I take it you didn't notice the bomb, then?

Bomb?
?

BEEP BEEP BEEP BEEP
02:05
BEEP BEEP BEEP BEEP

In two minutes, this mountain lair will be reduced to rubble.
You don't have enough time to fight me, save the kittens AND escape.
BEEP BEEP BEEP
02:03
BEEP BEEP BEEP
Face it, Mole. You have to let me go.

Let me think
about that.
Hmm …

… no.

What do you
mean, 'no?'

Bug—
defuse the
bomb.

I came here to kick butt and eat earthworms . . .

. . . and I'm all out of earthworms.

?
LET'S ROCK AND MOLE!

BOING!
FLIP!
PEW!
PEW!

WHOOSH!
WHOOSH!

POK
POK

???

Suction darts? Is this some kind of joke?
Most people find my sense of humour rather . . .

BEEP BEEP BEEP BEEP BEEP

BOOM
BOOM

CLANG!
BANG!
. . . disarming.

POW!
POW!
POW!
POK!
POK!
POK
BOOM
BOOM
BOOM
BOOM

CRASH!

LEAP!
Nudie,
Nudie,
Nudie.

Looks like you
don't have a leg
to stand on.

BZZZZZ
It's just a
flesh wound.
BZZZZ
BZZZZ
BZZZZ

CLICK

CLICK

No!
This wasn't part of the plan!

GRAB!
CRUNCH!

It was inevitable.
Dr Nude always triumphs!

Muhahahaa—

—hang on.
Who are they?

Them?
Oh, they're the *judges*.
From The Agency.

Judges?
What are you talking about?

Well, technically, Bug, Helena and I are not proper secret agents yet. We're still in training.

...

I'm sorry, ***what?!***

When you're a trainee spy you get three test missions.
Once you complete a mission successfully, you get your secret agent licence.

You cannot be serious.
I am serious. You're our very first mission.
So if we defeat you today, we pass the test!
And not to blow our own trumpets or anything, but I think we're doing pretty well so far.

What do you
reckon, judges? A+?
Top of the class?

SCRIBBLE
SCRIBBLE
SCRIBBLE

Come on, Nudie, be a sport and give up. Just this once.
Excuuuuse me?!
This can't be happening.
AAA-AAA-AAA...
We'd really appreciate it.
Would it help if I said please?

You're saying The Agency sent a bunch of... of... *trainees* to take me down?!
Me—the mighty Dr Nude?!
Were all the proper secret agents on holidays or something?
That's correct.
Umm, yes, they were, actually.
CHOO!

Never have I been so insulted, so disrespected . . .
I don't have to put up with this. I'm leaving.
CRASH!
CRASH!
Wait, let's talk about this—
WHOA!

Nudie,
come back!
MIAOW MIAOW MIAOW MIAOW MIAOW MIAOW MIAOW
No. I'm worth
more than this.
You've actually really
hurt my feelings.

Good day
to you.
ESCAPE
TUBE

SHUNK!
ESCAPE
TUBE

Who knew a naked mole rat would have such thin skin?

I never doubted you for a second— or even two.
I wonder how Helena got on with the kittens?

Dey're fibe.
SNIFF!

Then it's official:
mission accomplished!
Great job, team.
A-CHOO! Max,
Dr Nude got away!
AA-CHOO!

True . . . but
we still did *some*
good today.
That's got to be
worth something,
eh, judges?

Like
I said . . .
. . . top of
the class.
Hehe.

CHAPTER TWO:
FROZEN ASSETS

Ladies and gentlemen,
this is a robbery.

Freeze!

You first.
SQUIRT

SPLASH

I'm stuck. I'M STU—

EEK!
NOOOO!
GASP!
Nobody move!
SQUIRT
SQUIRT

All your gold belongs to us! Muhahahahahaa!

CHAPTER THREE:
OTHER FISH TO FRY

Sir.
Hello, W.
About the
mission . . .
W

Hold that thought, Max.
I've finally come up with
a better name for
The Agency.

Are you sure, sir?
With respect, your other ideas didn't exactly strike fear into the hearts of evildoers everywhere.

Give him a chance, Helena. I'm sure this time it will be excellent.
I think so, Max. From now on, we will be called . . .

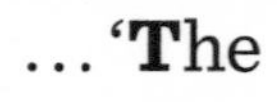

… '**T**he
Official
International
League
Exterminating
Terrorism'.

...

Oh dear.

Helena,
you're right!
Hmm.
'Hello, I'm Max Mole,
agent of TOILET' ...
... hardly makes
one feel *flushed*
with pride, W.

Now you mention it, it doesn't *bowl* me over either.
I got the idea while I was on the loo—perhaps that explains it.

So . . . the test results?
Ah, yes, of course. Let's see what the judges had to say, shall we?
W

JUNE BUG

Teeny-tiny tech support.

EQUIPMENT OF CHOICE:

* radar dish
* camera
* toolkit

SPECIAL SKILLS/QUALIFICATIONS:

* flying
* hacking
* lock-picking
* bomb-defusing
* surveillance
* champion cake baker

WEAKNESSES:

* bug spray
* rolled-up newspaper
* those zappy-zappy bug-light things

JUNE BUG

RESULTS: DEFUSED BOMB UNDER PRESSURE. EXCELLENT WORK.

HELENA HIPPO

Dependable. Determined. Deadly.

EQUIPMENT OF CHOICE:

* fists (nicknames: Ruth + Rita)
* legs (nickname: the ol' kicksticks)
* teeth (no nicknames, they're just teeth)

SPECIAL SKILLS/QUALIFICATIONS:

* amateur wrestling champion (alter ego: 'Helena Handbasket')
* punching things
* kicking things
* biting things
* punching + kicking + biting things at the same time
* putting up with Max

WEAKNESSES:

* allergic to cats

RESULTS: RISKED LIFE TO SAVE KITTENS. EXCELLENT WORK.

MAXIMILIAN 'MAX' MOLE

MAX

His granny loves him.
Earthworms fear him.
Villains find him ...
kind of annoying.

EQUIPMENT OF CHOICE:

* explosive suction-cup dart gun (aka 'Mr Boom-Boom')
* classy, dirt-repellent suit (white)

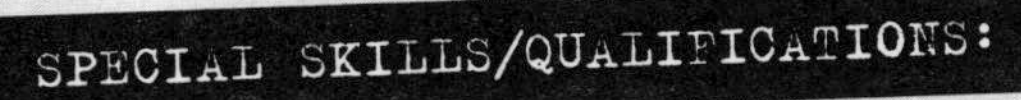

SPECIAL SKILLS/QUALIFICATIONS:

* expert marksman
* expert tunneller
* master of disguise
* snappy dresser
* expert bad-joke teller
* holds the world-record for eating the most earthworms in one hour

WEAKNESSES:

* does not plan ahead
* tells bad jokes
* easily distracted by earthworms

RESULTS: ALLOWED DR NUDE TO ESCAPE.

You three did your best going up against Dr Nude.
But, unfortunately, your best wasn't quite good enough.
The judges decided that you failed the test.
Oh *mud*. Well, we did our best, right team?

More specifically,
they say *you* failed, Max.
Me?
Uhhh . . .

Where is it? Ah, yes.
'Bug and Helena passed with flying colours, but Max let the team down. And because *he* failed, the *whole team* failed.'
Oh.
Right.

They said, and I quote, 'If Max Mole had planned ahead then he could have captured Dr Nude, and the whole team would have passed the test.
But instead, the whole. Team. Failed. Because. Of. *Him*.'
Yes, I . . . I think they've made their point. Thanks, W.
W

Cheer up, you still have two more goes at the test.
I'm sorry, team. I won't fail us again. Next time, I'll be ready; I'll plan for every possibility.

That's the spirit, Max. And you'll get your chance.
I have another mission for you.

INTERPOL need our help with an urgent case.
Chekhov will explain.

CHAPTER FOUR:
INSPECT THE GADGETS

So, got any new gadgets for me?
Here, have some tracking devices.
They always come in handy.

Thanks, but . . . I was hoping for something that explodes!
Uh, sure. Have my pen.

Does it explode?
If you squeeze it hard enough.

SQUEEZE

SPLURT

I see.
Or rather, I don't.

Trainees, The First Bank of New York was robbed an hour ago.
Here's the security footage.
Recognise anyone?

That's
Eric Goldfishfinger,
criminal mastermind!
He's mad
about gold.

And that's Toxin, the
most poisonous pufferfish
on the planet.

Correct.
They stole $10 million
in gold bars from the bank
vault, armed with nothing
but water pistols.

But weren't those two locked up in the maximum-security aquarium?
They broke out three days ago.

How did they escape? Did they *scale* the walls?
Max . . .

It's completely overcrowded, you know; really stuffed to the *gills*.
MAX.

They pack the prisoners in like *sardines*—especially the sardines.
MAX!

Sorry, you're right. No more jokes.
So why are the customers just standing there? Something fishy's going on.

It turns out the water pistols contained Toxin's *paralyzing pufferfish poison.*
The customers are all still alive, thankfully—they're just unable to move.

Is there an antidote for the poison?
I'm working on it.
Unfortunately not, Bug—we can't tell when *or* where they'll strike next.
But as soon as they surface, we'll hear about it.
GURGLE

So, trainees, you have your mission: catch these fiendish fish.
Roger that, W. Perhaps there's time to buy some fresh, yummy earthworms on the way?
As bait for the fish, of course. *Definitely* not for me.
W
Sorry, Max, the earthworms will have to wait . . .

ABC
ABC
ANIMAL BROADCAST CORPORATION
BREAKING NEWS – ROBBERY AT 2ND BANK
POLICE
... the fish are robbing another bank *right now*!

CHAPTER FIVE:
TANKS A LOT
SECOND BANK OF NEW YORK, NEW YORK CITY, NY, USA.
We're too late!
There's a flood in there. Talk about bursting the banks.
SCREECH!
BRM·82
ABC
EWS

NYP
POLICE
NYPD
POLICE
NYPD
POLICE

But why is there a hole in the building?
No idea. I'll look into it.

BOING!
BOING!
BOING!
BRM·82

Looks like Goldie and Toxin took the gold from this bank too.
The customers are all stuck, but luckily their heads are above water.

Max, Bug,
over here!

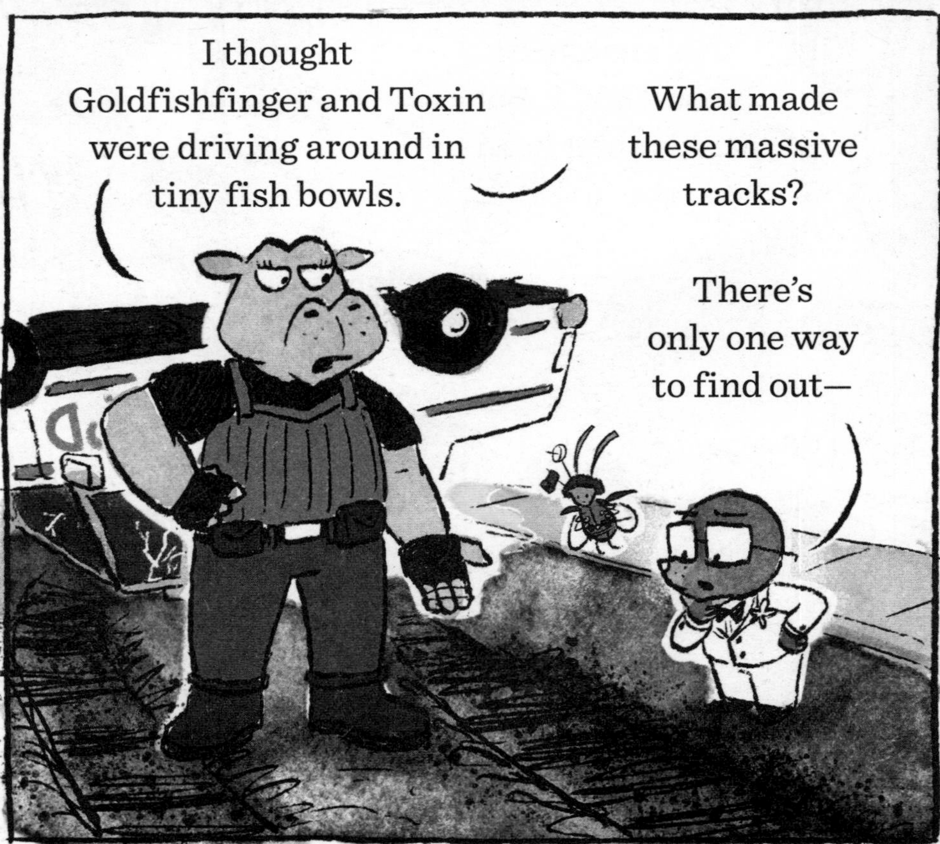
I thought
Goldfishfinger and Toxin
were driving around in
tiny fish bowls.
What made
these massive
tracks?
There's
only one way
to find out—

—let's track
them down.

A FEW BLOCKS AWAY . . .

Tremble, citizens of New York, before our fearsome
FISH TANK!
Muhahahaa!

Prepare to be paralysed!
Toxin, fire at will.
RUMBLE

RUMBLE ...
SQUIRT!
...RUMBLE RUMBLE RUMBLE
BONK

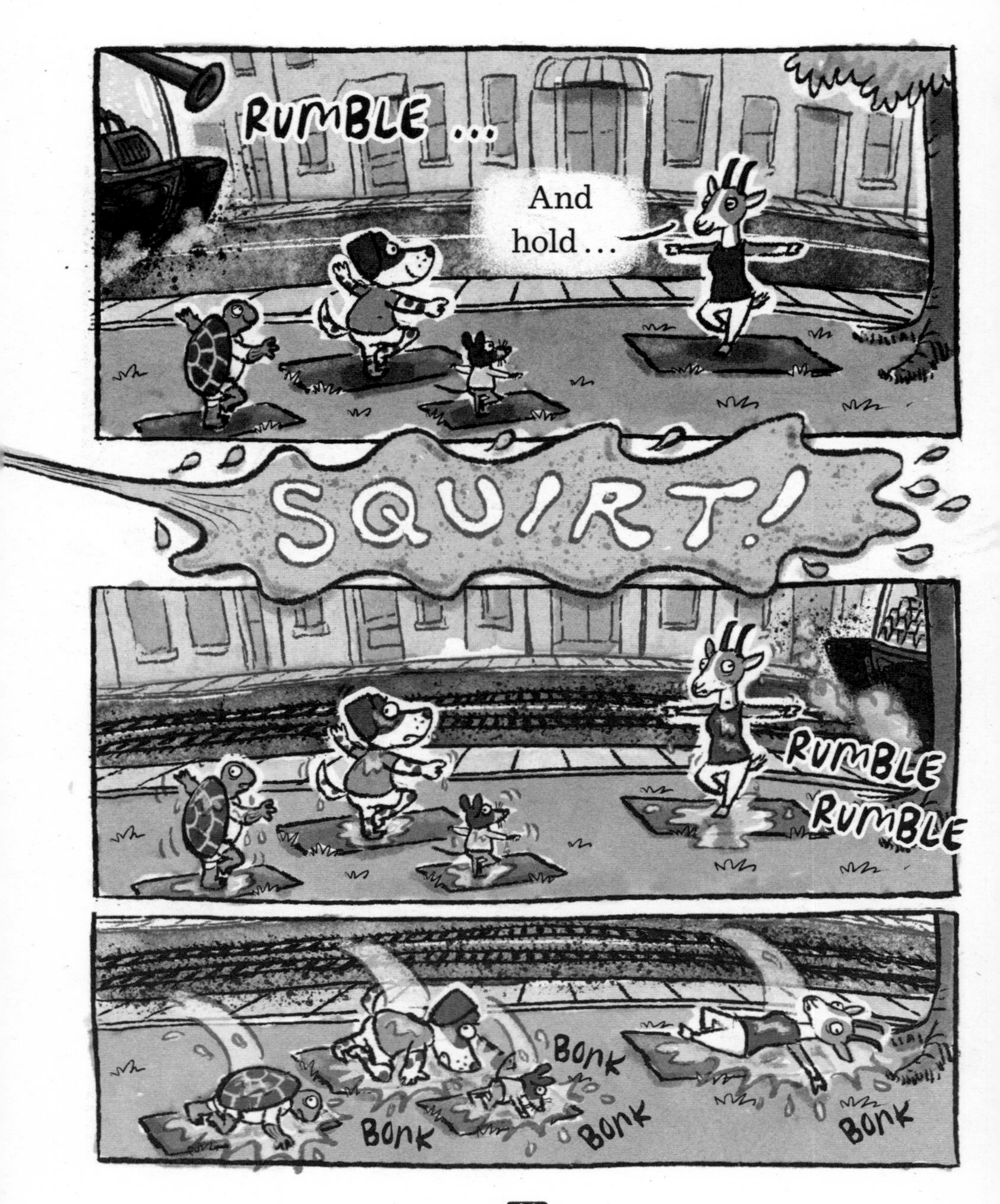
RUMBLE ...
And hold ...
SQUIRT!
RUMBLE
RUMBLE
BONK
BONK
BONK
BONK

RUMBLE ...
LIVING STATUE
SQUIRT!
RUMBLE
RUMBLE
Tink
Tink
LIVING STATUE

RUMBLE
SWERVE!
TAXI
There they are! What's the plan, Max?
BRM-82

Helena, take the wheel.
WHOA!

I'll blast open the glass with suction darts.

Bug, if that doesn't work, try to hack into the tank's electronics and shut it down.

I agree . . . that *actually* sounds like a plan.

Time to blow them out of the water.

PEW!
PEW!
PEW!

Huh?
POK!
POK!
POK!
How's my driving?
Call
1800-GLDFSHFNGR

BOOM
BOOM BOOM
Call
BRM·82

This is it, team! The moment we've been waiting for.
We're about to catch those fish and pass this test.

Prepare to become *proper* secret agents!

Is that all you've got?
Wait, what?

MUHAHAHAA!
How's my driving?
Call
1800-GLDFSH
GASP!

The Fish Tank is made of *bomb-proof glass*. Did you really think it would be that easy to stop us?
You must be wet behind the ears.
Speaking of which . . .

. . . never bring a convertible to a water fight.

SWIVEL!
How's my driving
Call
1800 - GLDFSHF
Oh
mud.

SQUIRT!

I'm stu—
Me t—

Like
shooting fish
in a barrel.
Muhahahahaa!

ZOOOOM
SCREECH!
Ta-ta, whoever you are!

CHAPTER SIX: **CRASH COURSE**

DRINK CROAKA COLA
STARDUCKS
ZOOM!

CLICK
Downloading HackPad System Update 2.5.03.
We'll let you know when it's ready! :)
BRM·82
BUMP!

CRASH!
TARA'S
TAR
TARA'S
TAR

It's
tar-iffic!

It's
tar-iffic!

SPLAT

SMASH!
HEADS DOWN
PILLOW FACTORY

HEADS DOWN
PILLOW FACTORY

COUGH!

Our feather-filled pillows are all they're quacked up to be!
Our feather-filled pillows are all they're quacked up to be!
fluff!

The Chainsaw-
Juggling Crocodile
and Knife-Throwing
Porcupine Club
(A club for crocodiles that
like to juggle chainsaws,
and also porcupines that
like to throw knives.)
Do not
enter
Do not
enter
!!!
BRM-82
ZOOOM!!

POKE! BITE! CHOMP!
STAB! NEEOW!
SMASH!
CRASH!
!

ZOOOM!
Still updating HackPad.
Thanks for waiting!

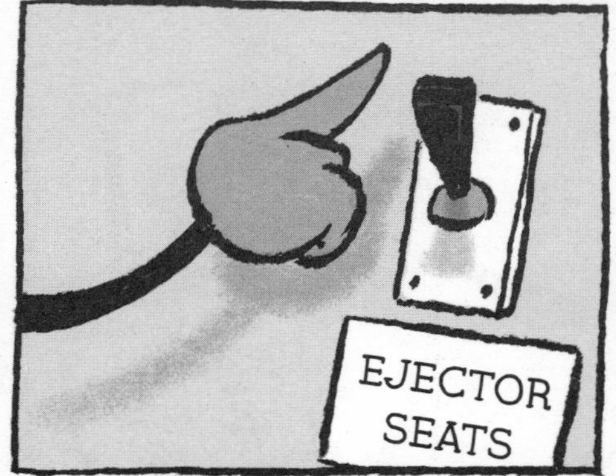
EJECTOR
SEATS

CLICK
EJECTOR
SEATS

?

CLICK
EJECTOR SEATS

CLICK
EJECTOR SEATS

CLICK
EJECTOR SEATS

CLICK
EJECTOR SEATS

CLICK CLICK CLICK
EJECTOR

???

ZOOOOM!

DiNG!

HackPad System Update 2.5.03 complete.
You're up-to-date!
Have a great day! :)

~~The Agency~~
~~Vehicle Computer Access Port~~

Username: BUG
Password: ********

~~Access Granted~~

BUG/>
TURN ENGINE OFF
~~Engine turned off~~

BUG/>
ACTIVATE BRAKES 100%

~~Brakes activated 100%~~

SCREECH!

HISSSSSSSS...

WHOOOOOOOSH!
WHOOOOOOOSH!
!
BANG!
BANG!

THUD
THUD

CHAPTER SEVEN:
IN FINE FEATHER

KSSHH!

KSSHH!

Wait for it . . .

GASP!
COUGH!

Where are those fish? Wait till I get a hold of them . . .
I've never felt so *down* in the mouth.

Trainees!
I'm so glad you're
all right.
We'd be at the
bottom of the bay if it
wasn't for Bug!

And we'd still be
stuck if it weren't
for Chekhov.
Whatever
you gave us did
the trick.

It's my brand-new, long-lasting antidote to Toxin's poison.
Thanks to this, he won't be able to paralyse you ever again.

You made a *paralysing-pufferfish-poison prevention potion*?
Pretty much. Bug, you'd better have some too.
KSSHH!

What about all the others who've been paralysed so far?

My team is making a massive batch of the antidote as we speak.
We'll have all the frozen citizens fixed up ASAP.
You're a legend, Chekhov. That's great news.
Indeed. But now for the bad news ...

... because Goldfishfinger and Toxin escaped, the judges say you've failed your secret agent test for a second time.

But, W, how were we to know they'd have a massive tank?
A secret agent must plan ahead for all possibilities.

So, trainees, you've got one chance left to pass the test.
Find Goldfishfinger and Toxin—and make sure you *capture them* this time.

We need to predict Goldfishfinger's next move.
He'll be after more gold. Which bank will he target next?
Hmm . . .

SEE THE PRICELESS
SOLID GOLD
FISH FINGER
A NEW ARTWORK by ANDY WARTHOG
GRAND OPENING TONIGHT
@THE MET, NYC
What if he doesn't attack a bank?

CHAPTER EIGHT:
TAKE THE BAIT

THE METROPOLITAN MUSEUM OF ART,
(AKA 'THE MET') NEW YORK CITY, NY, USA.

Anderson Coop here for Channel 5 News, coming to you live from The Met tonight . . .
. . . as New York's rich and famous gather for the opening of Andy Warthog's latest art extravaganza.
55

'Marilyn Monrodent'

'The Screaming Goat'

'The Trickery of Imagery'

32 paintings of Camel's Soup

'Plain White Canvas #63'
(from the 'Overpriced
Nonsense' series)
$3 MILLION
'Giant Toilet
with Water Lilies'
(aka 'Ripples in
the Pond #2')

And last but not least, the priceless

SOLID GOLD FISH FINGER

Bug, we have eyes on the fish finger.
Are you in position?

ELSEWHERE ...

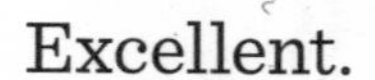

Time to put one of Chekhov's tracking devices on the golden fish finger—

—just in case the villains somehow get away with it.

I'm planning ahead, you see.
What do you think of that, eh, judges?

Good job,
Max.
Thank you.
And may I say,
you look lovely in your
disguise this evening.
BUMP

Aw, shucks. You've looked better,
though—Chekhov's pen has
leaked in your pocket.
GASP!

My favourite shirt! It's ruined—
SNIFF SNIFF

Ooh, earthworm quiche! I'll be right back . . .

MEANWHILE . . .
So, Andy—how did you get the idea for the priceless, solid gold fish finger?
Were you thinking about consumerism?
The obesity epidemic?
The overfishing of our oceans?
Nah . . .

. . . I was just
really hungry and
thinking about
fish fingers.

Muhahahahaa!
CRASH!

Camel's
YOU'LL NEVER SPIT THIS OUT!
SOUP
AAAAARGHH
Is this the drive-through? I'll have one priceless, solid gold fish finger . . . to go.

Sorry to
put a dampener
on your evening.

SPLASH!
EEK

It's just a simple robbery, folks. No cause for alarm.

I beg to differ.
FIRE ALARM

FIRE ALARM
CLICK

PSSSSHH
PSSSSHH

PSSSSHH
PSSSSHH

GASP!

How are they unstuck? This isn't the plan!
What's going on?
AAARGHH!

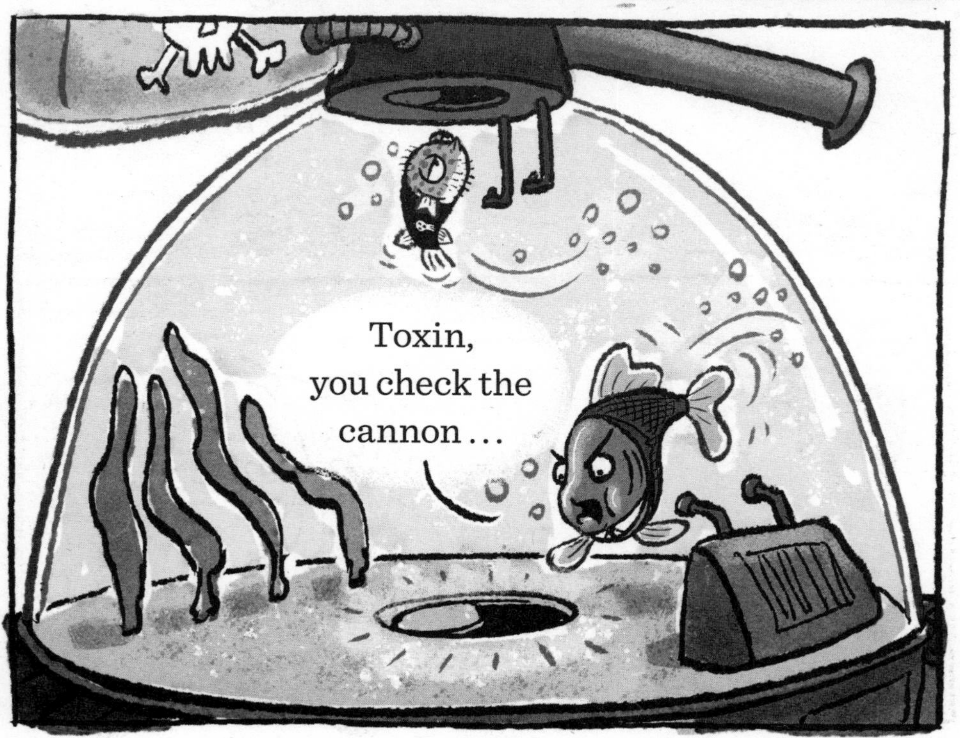
Toxin, you check the cannon . . .

... while
I grab ...
... the gold
fish finger!
Muhahahaa!

Not my fish finger!

Beat it, beatnik!
EEP!

AAAAAA!

It's more beautiful than I ever imagined. And it's all mine!

Excuse me, sir—no touching the artwork.
You!

Huh—
YOINK

BIFF
BAM
Splash

Grrr, it's the mole and the hippo!
Hello again, Goldie.

So you survived your little joyride …
… AND you found an antidote for Toxin's poison.
Sure did. Bug put it in the fire sprinkler system.
Sorry to pour cold water over your plans.
Now tell me …

... is this little bowl bomb-proof?

Of course! But here's a more pressing question ...

Camel's
SOUP
Camel's
SOUP
RUMBLE

... are your bodies tank-proof?
Camel's
YOU'LL NEVER SPIT THIS OUT!
SOUP
Camel's
YOU'LL NEVER SPIT THIS OUT!
SOUP

CHAPTER NINE:
BOWLED OVER

CRASH!

Ow, my bum.

CONK
OOF!

Camel's
SOUP
Uh-oh.
RUMBLE

Time for a quick, underground getaway!
LEAP!

SPLAT

Ugh ...
the floor was a *teensy bit* more solid than I expected.

Umm, Bug? Helena?
Any advice for stopping a bomb-proof tank?
RUMBLE

IN THE AIR VENTS . . .

Don't worry, Bug, just get here as soon as you can—I'll save Max.

Now what can I use to stop a tank?
Hang on a sec . . .

... the fish finger.
But it was supposed to be solid gold.

I lied. It's solid steel covered in gold paint!
I'm a fraud. SOB! My artworks are built on lies and nonsense!
Did you say solid steel?

Helena?

A little . . .

. . . HELP!
Coming!

You wanted
the fish finger?
You got it!

SHUNK!

CRUNCH!
POP!

THUD!

Helena! You just stopped a tank in its tracks . . . using a giant fish finger!
All in a day's work.
Keep an eye on Toxin. I'll find Goldfishfinger—

Not if I find you first!
SMACK!

I've got you now, Mole.
You can't escape my clutches . . .

That's what
you think!
WRIGGLE
WRIGGLE

Haha!
SHOOP

SPLAT
Get off, Mole!
I can't see where I'm going . . .
You don't want to know.

Oh
mud.
CRASH!

BONK
SPLASH

SLAM

You can lead a mole to water …
… but can you make him drown?
Muhahahahaa!

CHAPTER TEN:
HUFF AND PUFF

Oh no,
what have
I done?
Poor little
pufferfish.
I must've
scared him
to death.

Do I give him
mouth-to-mouth?
Gross . . .

YIKES!
PUFF
SPLATCH!
OOF!

Whoa!
SPLASH!

SPLOING
SPLOING

SPURT

Hey!
Come back here, you puffed-up bag of wind!

CLACK

Bug!
Don't let him get to the fish bowl!

WHACK!

POP!
WHOOSH

SPLOING
SPLOING
WHOOOOOOOOOOOOOSHHHHH!!

SPLUMF

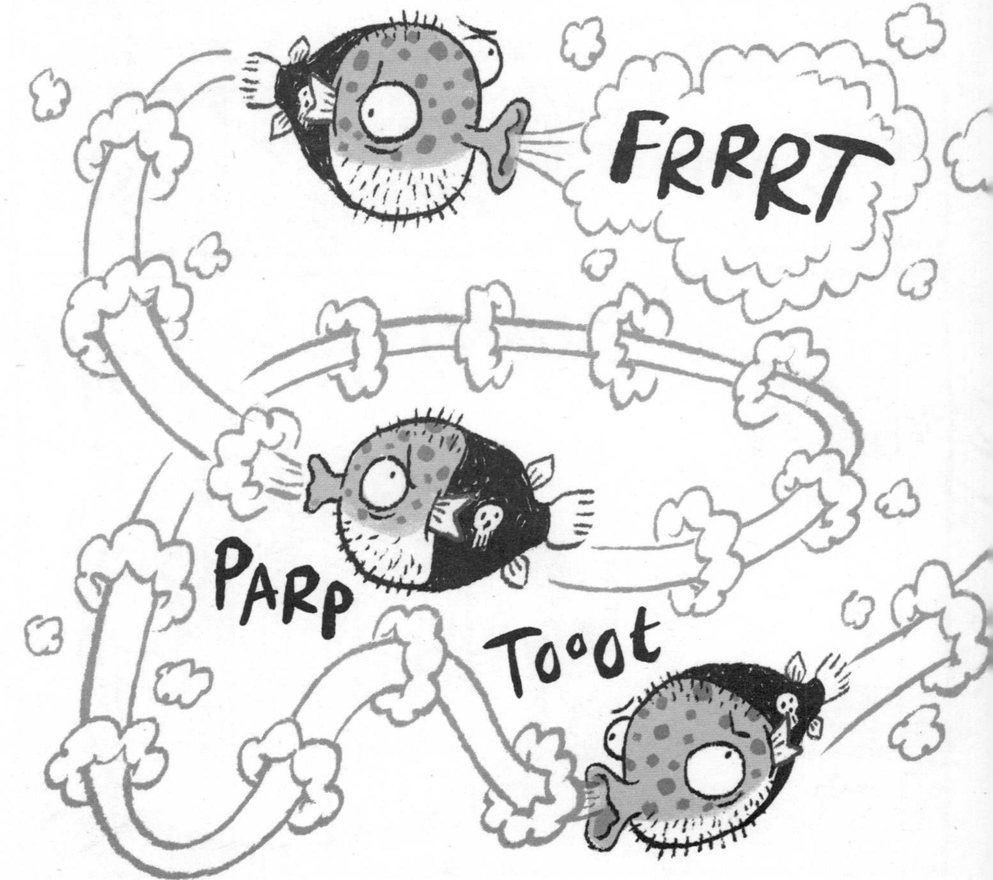
FRRRT
PARP
Tooot

PoOot
PtHLBFtH
SPLAT
$3 MILLION

You're a champion, Bug!
$5 MILLION

SCHLEEP
$5 MILLION

$5 MILLION

Splash

$5 MILLION
LIFT

Don't go anywhere.

Hey, Bug, where's Max?

Max, come in. Do you have Goldfishfinger?
Max?!

CHAPTER ELEVEN:
DOWN THE TOILET

SPLURT!

YEARRGH!

SQUIRT

Bug!
Helena!
I'm in the loo!

Max?!
Helena! Bug! Am I glad to see you.

Are you OK?
I'm fine. But if it weren't for **Chekhov's pen,** my career would've been down the toilet.

And Goldfishfinger?
Trapped. He's the catch of the day!

Think again!
LEAP!

CLICK
FLUSH

See you around the bend!
FLUSH
GURGLE
Muhahahahaa!

SCRIBBLE
SCRIBBLE
SCRIBBLE

So ... that's it, then.
We failed the secret agent test three times.
It's over.
It's not *quite* over yet, Helena. You see ...
... I planned ahead!

A WATER PIPE
EAST RIVER, NEW YORK

Haha, freedom!

What? Unhand me!
SNATCH!

No!

NO! It's not possible.
Sure it is!

While we were fighting in the loo, I slipped a tracking device in your pocket.
I don't believe it!

Believe it, Goldie . . . you've been caught by the agents of TOILET.
Max . . .

CHAPTER TWELVE:
WATER UNDER THE BRIDGE

Toxin and Goldfishfinger are on their way back to the maximum-security aquarium.
We retrieved all the stolen gold, and the frozen citizens have made full recoveries.
Plus, Andy Warthog has discovered a new painting technique.

SPLAT

Everything's wrapped up nicely.
Indeed. Now, about your test results.

The judges were very impressed with all of you . . .
I knew it! We passed!

. . . *however,* they are not prepared to give you your secret agent licences . . .
. . . until you tie up the loose ends from your first mission.
What?
PARDON?!

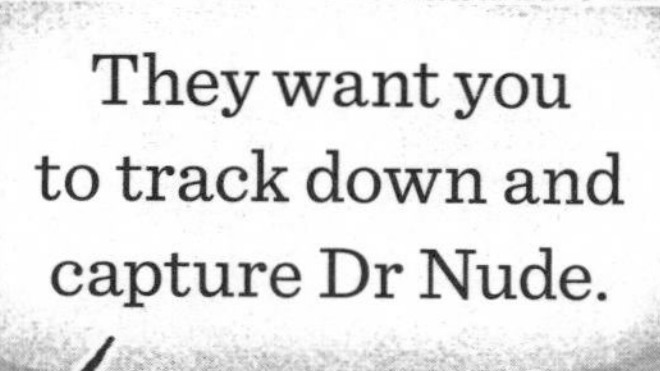

They want you to track down and capture Dr Nude.
Not him again. He's so grumpy … and so naked.

Yesterday, STAR Division discovered a meteorite with anti-gravity powers. Dr Nude wants to steal it for his evil plans.
And let me guess— the judges said this situation is all my fault because I let Dr Nude get away.

I do believe they did. Yes, here it is …
'… as usual, this is all Max Mole's fault.'

The judges have made it very clear . . .
. . . if you three can stop Dr Nude from stealing the meteorite and bring him to justice, you'll be made full secret agents.
So . . . are you ready for your next mission?

Does my granny make the world's best earthworm pie?

You bet she does.

LET'S ROCK AND MOLE!